Ladybird  F

Let's Paint!

To access the audio and digital versions
of this book:

1 Go to **www.ladybirdeducation.co.uk**
2 Click "Unlock book"
3 Enter the code below

gEKxsJcPUq

Notes to teachers, parents, and carers

The *Ladybird Readers* Beginner level helps young language learners to become familiar with key conversational phrases in English. The language introduced has clear real-life applications, giving children the tools to hold their first conversations in English.

This book focuses on asking the question "What does he paint?" and provides practice of saying colors such as "blue", "yellow", and "red" in English. The pictures that accompany the text show a range of settings, which may be used to introduce one or two pieces of topic-based vocabulary, such as "paper" and "class", if the children are ready.

There are some activities to do in this book. They will help children practice these skills:

 Speaking    Listening*   Writing   Reading   Singing*

*To complete these activities, listen to the audio downloads available at **www.ladybirdeducation.co.uk**

Series Editor: Sorrel Pitts   Text adapted by Hazel Geatches   Song lyrics by Wardour Studios

LADYBIRD BOOKS

UK | USA | Canada | Ireland | Australia
India | New Zealand | South Africa

Ladybird Books is part of the Penguin Random House group of companies whose addresses can be found at global.penguinrandomhouse.com.
www.penguin.co.uk   www.puffin.co.uk   www.ladybird.co.uk

Penguin
Random House
UK

First published 2021
001

Printed in China
A CIP catalogue record for this book is available from the British Library
ISBN: 978-0-241-44011-7

All correspondence to:
Ladybird Books
Penguin Random House Children's
One Embassy Gardens, 8 Viaduct Gardens, London SW11 7BW

FSC
www.fsc.org

MIX
Paper from
responsible sources
FSC® C018179

Ladybird 🐞 Readers

Let's Paint!

Based on the Learning Time with Timmy TV series
created in partnership with the British Council

Watch the original episode "Rainbow Colours" online.

Picture words

Timmy

Yabba

Ruffy

rainbow   sky

tractor

Timmy has some blue paint.

What does he paint?

Timmy paints blue sky.

Yabba gives Timmy some
yellow paint.

What does Timmy paint now?

12

Timmy paints a yellow sun.

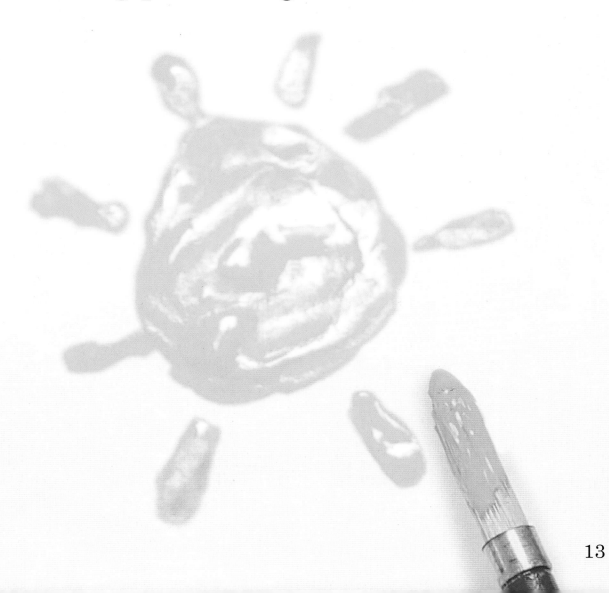

Ruffy gives Timmy some red paint.

What does Timmy paint now?

Timmy paints a red tractor.

Then, Timmy paints a rainbow!

The picture is great.
Well done, Timmy!

Your turn!

1 Talk with a friend.

What does Timmy paint?

Timmy paints a tractor.

What color is the tractor?

It is red.

20

2 What color? Listen. Circle the words.

1      green   (blue)

2      orange   yellow

3      yellow   red

4      blue   green

3 **Listen. Put a** ☑ **by the correct words.**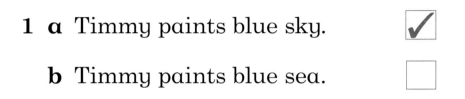

1 a Timmy paints blue sky. ✓

  b Timmy paints blue sea. ☐

2 a Timmy paints a yellow sun. ☐

  b Timmy paints a yellow flower. ☐

3 a Timmy paints a green tractor. ☐

  b Timmy paints a red tractor. ☐

4 a The picture is good. ☐

  b The picture is great. ☐

4 Listen. Write the first letters.

1

tractor

2

sun

3

paint

5 **Sing the song.** 🔊

Timmy has some blue paint so he can try
To paint a picture of a big blue sky.
The picture is great. Well done!
Timmy, Timmy paints a yellow sun.

Timmy, Timmy paints a rainbow!
Blue, red, yellow—this is fun!

Timmy has some red paint. What is that for?
Timmy, Timmy paints a red tractor.
Tractor and sky and rainbow and sun.
The picture is great. Well done!

Timmy, Timmy paints a rainbow!
Blue, red, yellow—this is fun!